Appleville Elementary

Fooled You!

Be sure to read all of the books about
Appleville Elementary School!

Appleville Elementary

Fooled You!

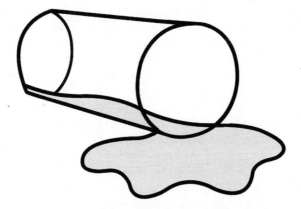

by **Nancy Krulik**
illustrated by **Bernice Lum**

SCHOLASTIC INC.
New York   Toronto   London   Auckland
Sydney   Mexico City   New Delhi   Hong Kong

For my dad,
the ultimate nature counselor.

ISBN 978-0-545-11776-0

Text copyright © 2010 by Nancy Krulik
Illustrations copyright © 2010 by Scholastic Inc.
All rights reserved.
Published by Scholastic Inc.
SCHOLASTIC, LITTLE APPLE, and associated logos are trademarks
and/or registered trademarks of Scholastic Inc.

12 11 10 9 8 7 6 5 4 3 2   11 12 13 14 15/0

Printed in the U.S.A.   40
First printing, March 2010
Book design by Yaffa Jaskoll

Chapter 1
Who's the Caboose?

Justine wiggled to the left. She wiggled to the right. Then she bounced all around.

"You can't sit still," Marika said.

"I'm excited," Justine replied.

"Why?" Marika asked.

"Miss Popper is moving the job wheel," Justine said.

Marika understood. The first graders all liked having classroom jobs.

"I hope I'm line leader," Justine said. "I like being first."

"I like being line leader, too," Albert told Justine.

"You were line leader *last* week," Carlos reminded Albert. "You can't have the same job this week."

"Then I want to be the caboose," Albert said.

The caboose was last in line. The caboose got to hold the door for the whole class.

"The caboose is cool," J.B. said.

"Okay," Miss Popper said. "This week our line leader is Marika."

Marika clapped. "Yes!" she cheered.

"And Justine will be our caboose," Miss Popper said.

"Toot! Toot!" Justine sounded just like a little train.

Miss Popper looked back at the job wheel. "J.B. will be our energy saver," she said.

J.B. sat up, tall and proud. Being energy saver was an important job. He had to make sure the lights were off when the class left the room.

"This week, you're the paper passer," Miss Popper told Albert.

That did not make Albert happy. Paper passer was the worst job on the wheel. All you did was pass out worksheets. Still, it was only for one week.

"And Carlos is our zookeeper," Miss Popper said.

Carlos grinned. He liked being

zookeeper. He got to give food and water to the five classroom gerbils.

"Zookeeper is going to be a big job this week," Miss Popper told Carlos. "We will be getting some new pets today."

Wow! That was very exciting news! The kids all started talking.

"What kind of pets?" Marika asked.

"How many pets?" Carlos wondered.

"Will they have fur, feathers, or fins?" Albert asked.

"Will they be boy pets or girl pets?" J.B. wanted to know.

"Will we be allowed to bring them home on the weekends?" Justine asked.

"You have all asked very good questions," Miss Popper told them. "And you will get your answers. But not until after lunch."

Chapter 2
April Fool!

The new pets were all the first graders talked about during lunch.

"I bet we're getting fish," Albert said. "My big brother told me they had a fish tank when he was in first grade."

"I don't care what kind of pets they are," Carlos said. "I'm just glad I get to take care of them."

"I wish I were zookeeper this week," Marika said.

"I wish I were anything except paper

passer," Albert told her. "You're line leader. That's a good job."

Marika nodded. Albert was right. Being line leader made her happy. But her empty lunch box did not.

"I'm still hungry," she said.

"Do you want my apple?" Justine asked.

"Sure," Marika said. "Thanks."

Marika took a big bite of Justine's apple. She chewed and chewed. And then she spit out the chewed-up apple.

"Yuck!" Marika shouted.

"What's wrong?" Albert asked her.

"There's a worm in this apple!" Marika said. She rubbed her tongue on a clean napkin.

Justine started laughing.

"It's not funny!" Marika yelled.

"Yes, it is," Justine said.

Albert looked at the apple. He pulled out half a worm.

"Yuck!" Marika shouted. "You touched a worm."

"You *ate* a worm," Carlos reminded her.

"Yuck!" Marika rubbed her tongue on the napkin again.

"It's okay," Albert said. "It's not a real worm. It's a gummy worm."

Justine laughed even harder. "Fooled you!" she told Marika.

"That wasn't nice," Marika said.

"It was a joke," Justine said. "Don't you know what day it is?"

"April first," J.B. said.

Justine nodded. "It's April Fools' Day," she explained. "You're *supposed* to play jokes on people today."

"I still don't want that apple," Marika said.

"I hope Miss Popper doesn't know it's April Fools' Day," Carlos said.

"Why not?" Albert asked.

"Because she could be fooling us about the new pets," Carlos told him.

"Miss Popper would never do that," J.B. said.

"I hope not," Carlos said. "Because I really want more class pets."

Chapter 3
Hello, New Pets

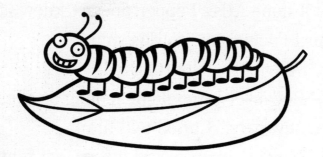

After lunch, Carlos raced down the hall. He couldn't wait to meet the new class pets.

"Carlos!" Marika shouted. "Stop! *I'm* the line leader. I go in the classroom first."

Carlos didn't want to wait. But he had to. Those were the rules.

Once he got into the room, Carlos ran to the corner. There was a net cage there. Inside the cage were five wiggly, squiggly insects. They were black, with white and yellow stripes.

"Worms?" Carlos asked. "Our class pets are *worms*?"

"Cool!" J.B. shouted.

"Gross!" Marika said. "I don't want to see any more worms."

"They're not worms," Albert told Marika. "Worm starts with a *W*. The sign on the cage starts with a *C*."

Carlos looked at the sign. "C-A-T," he read. "That spells cat."

"Those squiggly things are *not* cats," Marika said.

"They're caterpillars!" Albert told the class. Albert was a very good reader.

"You're right," Miss Popper said. "But they won't be caterpillars forever. They'll grow up to become butterflies."

"I love butterflies!" Marika said. "They're prettier than caterpillars."

"How does a caterpillar turn into a butterfly?" Carlos asked.

"It goes through many changes," Miss Popper said. "Everyone take your seats. Let's talk about our new pets."

The first graders rushed to sit down.

On the way to his chair, Albert saw a shiny dime. He bent down to pick it up.

But the dime was stuck to the floor. Albert pulled harder. The dime would not come up.

Rip!

"Uh-oh!" Albert said. "I ripped my pants."

"It's not a real dime," Justine told him. "It's a trick dime. It's glued to the floor.

You can't pick it up. April Fool!" She laughed really hard.

Albert did not laugh.

"Now I have to spend a whole afternoon with a rip in my pants," he said. "All because of your joke."

"Your joke was *mean*," J.B. told Justine.

"It's okay, Albert," Carlos said. "I have an extra pair of shorts in my cubby. You can borrow them."

"Thank you," Albert said.

"Justine, please say you're sorry to Albert," Miss Popper scolded.

"I'm sorry," Justine said. But she was still laughing.

"I'm glad April Fools' Day only comes once a year," Albert said.

The other first graders felt the exact same way. *Except Justine, of course.*

Chapter 4
Still Fooling!

On the day after April Fools' Day, Justine and J.B. had a playdate at J.B's house.

"Catch this!" J.B. called out. He threw a ball in the air.

Justine reached out her baseball glove. She ran for the ball.

Ruff! Ruff! J.B.'s dog, Frisky, ran, too. The ball fell right into his mouth.

"Hey!" Justine said. "J.B. threw that to *me*."

Frisky looked up at Justine. He wagged his tail.

"I'm tired of playing ball, anyway," Justine said.

"Me, too," J.B. agreed. "Let's go have a snack."

"I want to put my glove in my backpack," Justine told J.B.

"Okay," J.B. said. "Meet me in the kitchen."

J.B. and Justine were in the kitchen when they heard J.B.'s mom shout.

"FRISKY!" she called out.

The dog came running.

J.B.'s little brother, Mikey, came running.

J.B. and Justine came running, too.

"Bad dog," J.B.'s mom said.

Frisky looked up at her. He didn't know what he had done.

But Mikey knew. He pointed to the floor.

"Frisky spilled a cup of milk," he said.

"How did a cup of milk get into the hallway?" J.B. asked.

Ruff! Ruff! Frisky barked.

J.B.'s mom got paper towels from the kitchen. She started to clean up the spilled milk. Then she stopped.

"This isn't real," J.B.'s mom said. "This is plastic!"

Justine started laughing. "Fooled you!" she shouted. "Doesn't it look like real milk?"

J.B.'s mom frowned at Justine. Then she pet Frisky on the head.

"I'm sorry," J.B.'s mom said to the dog. "Do you want a treat?"

Frisky knew what *treat* meant. He wagged his tail.

"Why did you do that?" J.B. asked Justine. "It's not April Fools' Day anymore."

"I know," Justine said. "But I still like fooling people. That was funny."

"It wasn't funny for Frisky," J.B. said. "He almost got in trouble."

Justine shrugged. "It was funny to me," she said.

J.B.'s mom gave the cup with fake spilled milk back to Justine.

"I'll go put this in my backpack," Justine said.

"I think that's a good idea," J.B.'s mom said.

Soon, J.B., Justine, and Mikey were eating cookies in the kitchen. Everybody was happy again. Even Frisky.

"These sure are yummy cookies," Justine said.

Frisky barked. His treat was very yummy, too.

Mikey picked up his cup of juice. He took a sip. Then he stopped.

"Aaaaahh!" Mikey jumped up so fast that he knocked over his cup.

"Hey!" J.B. shouted. "You got juice all over me!"

"I'm sorry," Mikey said. "But there was a fly in my juice."

"Let me see," J.B. said.

He looked on the table. There was a fly sitting in a puddle of red juice. But it wasn't moving.

"This fly isn't real," J.B. said.

"Ha-ha," Justine chuckled. "Fooled you!"

"You're mean, Justine," Mikey said.

"No, I'm not," Justine said. "I'm funny."

"Mean Justine! Mean Justine!" Mikey chanted.

J.B.'s mom came running in. "What happened?" she asked.

"Justine played a trick on Mikey," J.B. said.

J.B.'s mom looked at the puddle of juice. She saw the stain on J.B.'s shirt.

J.B.'s mom went to the phone.

"Who are you calling?" Justine asked.

"Your mother," J.B.'s mom told her. "It's time for you to go home. There have been too many jokes today."

Chapter 5
Where Are the Caterpillars?

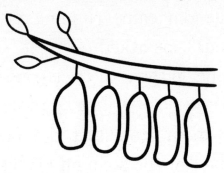

But Justine didn't stop playing jokes.

She gave J.B. a piece of candy that turned his mouth dark blue for two days!

She tricked Marika into chewing a piece of gum that tasted like pepper. Boy was Marika surprised!

But the *biggest* surprise came two weeks later. It was in the caterpillar cage.

"The caterpillars are gone!" Albert shouted.

"Did they get loose?" Carlos asked.

"There isn't a hole in the net," J.B. said.

Marika looked at Justine. "Did you take them? Is this one of your jokes?"

Justine shook her head. "I wouldn't do that. It wouldn't be funny."

"Then where are they?" Marika asked.

Miss Popper smiled. "Your pets are still here," she said. "Do you see the green cones hanging from the branches?"

The kids looked into the net cage. There were five green cones hanging from the branches.

"Those are called cocoons," Miss Popper said. "The caterpillars are inside."

"Who put the cocoons into the cage?" Marika asked.

"And how did the caterpillars get into the cocoons?" J.B. wondered. "Did they climb in?"

Miss Popper shook her head. "They didn't have to climb inside," she told the class. "All they had to do was shed their skin."

"Gross," Carlos said.

Miss Popper laughed. "It's not gross," she told him. "It's just what caterpillars do. They shed their old skin. Then the new skin becomes a hard cocoon. The cocoons protect the caterpillars while they turn into butterflies."

"How will they eat?" Albert asked. He needed to know. He was the zookeeper this week.

"They won't eat until they come out of their cocoons," Miss Popper explained.

"Will they be butterflies when they come out?" Marika asked.

Miss Popper held up a picture of an orange-and-black butterfly.

"They will look like this," she said.

"How pretty!" Marika said.

"Let me take a picture of you with the cocoons," Justine said to J.B.

"Okay," J.B. said.

Justine aimed her camera right at J.B. She pushed the button.

Whoosh. A big spray of water hit J.B. in the face.

"Fooled you!" Justine shouted out. "It's a trick camera."

"That wasn't funny," J.B. said.

"*I* thought it was," Justine told him.

She was the only one. Miss Popper and the first graders were very tired of Justine's jokes.

Chapter 6
Surprise!

Two weeks later there was another surprise waiting for the first graders.

"Butterflies!" Carlos shouted out happily as he ran into the classroom.

The butterflies had burst out of their cocoons. Everyone was very excited.

"I'm so glad I wore my orange tutu today," Marika said. "I match our butterflies."

"The butterflies are really cool," J.B. said.

"But that cage is too small," Albert said.

"That's true," Miss Popper agreed.

"Are we going to get them a bigger cage?" J.B. asked.

"No," Miss Popper said. "We're going to do something much better."

"What's that?" Carlos asked.

"We're going to set them free," Miss Popper told him.

Carlos didn't like that. "Then they won't be our pets anymore."

"No," Albert said. "But they'll be happier."

"Exactly," Miss Popper said.

"Where will we set them free?" J.B. asked.

"At the Ladybug Nature Center," Miss Popper answered. "We're going on a field trip."

"What's a nature center?" Albert asked.

"It's like a big park," Miss Popper said. "We'll take a hike. Then we'll learn all about the animals and plants that live there."

"When are we going?" J.B. asked.

"Tomorrow," Miss Popper said. "I will

give you field trip notes for your parents to sign."

"This calls for a snack!" Justine called out. "I have a can of pretzels in my backpack."

"Can we have some?" Marika asked Miss Popper.

"I think that would be okay," Miss Popper said.

"Great!" Justine cheered.

She handed Carlos a big can. It had pictures of pretzels all over it.

"Thanks," Carlos said.

He twisted the top off of the can and—*POP!* Three toy snakes sprang out of the can.

"Aaah!" Carlos shouted. He jumped backward.

Crash! Carlos knocked over the globe when he jumped.

"Ha-ha-ha!" Justine laughed. "Fooled you!"

Justine was the only one laughing. No one else thought her joke was funny. Not one bit.

Chapter 7
BUZZ!

The next morning, Justine was the first one to climb onto the field trip bus.

"How come you get to go first?" Carlos asked her.

"I'm the line leader this week," Justine told him. "I get to go first all week long."

Justine sat down near the front of the bus.

"I'm not sitting near you," Carlos told Justine. "I don't want any snakes jumping out at me."

"I'm not sitting near you, either, Justine," J.B. said. "I don't want blue lips again." He sat down across from Carlos.

"And I don't want to rip my pants again," Albert said. He sat next to Carlos.

"I don't want to sit with you, either," Marika told Justine.

"But we always sit together," Justine said to Marika. "We're best friends."

Marika shook her head. "You play too many mean jokes. I don't want to be your best friend."

"Justine, you will sit with me," Miss Popper said.

Justine didn't like that idea. Miss Popper was nice, but she was still a teacher.

Justine had no choice. She sat next to

Miss Popper the whole way to the Ladybug Nature Center. Lucky for Justine, it was a very short trip.

When the bus pulled into the nature center, a tall man in a big green hat walked over to greet the first graders.

"Hello," he said. "I'm Mr. Barker. Welcome to the Ladybug Nature Center."

The kids looked around. They saw trees and flowers.

"Where are the animals?" Carlos asked Mr. Barker.

"They're here," Mr. Barker said. "Some animals are hiding in the trees. Some are swimming in the lakes. And some are flying in the air."

"So there are lots of different animals?" Albert asked.

"Yes," Mr. Barker said. "You never know what you will find here. We're full of surprises."

Justine walked up to Mr. Barker. She put out her hand politely.

"I'm Justine," she said.

Mr. Barker smiled. He reached out to shake Justine's hand.

BUZZ!

Mr. Barker jumped back. Justine had just given him a big shock.

Justine turned over her hand. She was holding a buzzer.

"I'm full of surprises, too!" she told Mr. Barker. "Fooled you!"

"Justine!" Miss Popper said sternly. "That is *not* how a first grader acts."

"I'm sorry," Justine said. But she didn't sound like she really meant it.

"It's okay," Mr. Barker said to Justine. He didn't sound like *he* really meant it, either.

"We're going to hike around the nature center," Miss Popper told the class. "And then we'll set our butterflies free."

"You can also try to get through our giant maze," Mr. Barker said. "The paths are all marked with thick bushes."

"I don't want to be stuck in a maze with Justine," Carlos whispered to J.B.

"I'm tired of her jokes," Marika whispered to Albert.

"We have to make her stop," J.B. agreed.

Albert thought for a minute. Then he said, "I know a way to do that."

Marika, J.B., and Carlos all moved closer to Albert. They couldn't wait to hear his secret plan.

It was time to stop Justine's jokes!

Chapter 8
Spring into Spring!

A few minutes later, the first graders were hiking around the nature center.

"Oh, look!" Albert shouted. "A mother duck is swimming with her babies."

The class looked out at the lake. There was a duck family. Nearby were three turtles sitting on a log.

"I love turtles," Marika said. "But I hate turtleneck shirts. They make my neck itch. Do real turtles have itchy necks, Mr. Barker?"

Mr. Barker laughed. "I've never asked them," he told her.

The first graders followed Mr. Barker all around the nature center. They saw pretty flowers, tall trees, and a beautiful, red bird.

"That's a robin redbreast," Mr. Barker said. "When you see him, it's a sign that spring is here."

Carlos began to jump up and down.

"What are you doing?" Marika asked him.

"I'm springing!" Carlos said. "Boing. Boing."

"He didn't mean that kind of spring, silly," Marika said.

"I know," Carlos told her. "But it's fun. Try it."

All of the kids started to spring up and down. *Boing. Boing. Boing.*

Miss Popper laughed. So did Mr. Barker.

"This is a fun nature center," J.B. told Mr. Barker.

"Wait until you try the maze," Mr. Barker said. "It's the most fun of all."

The kids followed Mr. Barker down a long path. He stopped when they came to a big group of bushes.

"This is our maze," Mr. Barker said. "You'll start here. Then you'll walk through the paths until you find the way out."

"Let's go!" Albert shouted.

Albert started to run into the maze. But Justine stopped him.

"I'm the line leader," she said. "I'm going to lead the way."

Chapter 9
Which Way Do We Go?

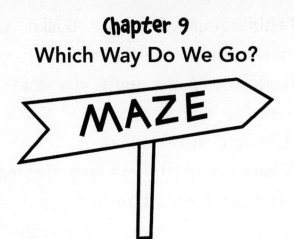

The maze was really twisty. It would be very hard not to get lost.

"We should turn to the right," Marika called up to Justine the line leader.

"No, to the left," Carlos said.

"I think we have to go straight," Albert said.

"Maybe we should go backward?" J.B. thought.

"Stop talking!" Justine yelled. "You're mixing me up."

Justine looked left. She looked right. Then she said, "Let's go left."

Justine looked straight ahead as she walked. She didn't turn around to ask her friends for help.

"I think we were here before," Marika called to Justine. "I know that bush."

"All the bushes look the same," Justine answered without turning around.

"I think I saw *that* bush before, too," J.B. said.

"I'm the leader," Justine said. "And I say we weren't here before."

"Okay, leader, which way should we go?" Carlos asked.

"Left," Justine said.

Justine went left. Then she turned right. And right again.

"I think I see the end," Justine

shouted back to the other kids. "It's over there."

"That doesn't look like the end," Carlos said.

"Are you sure?" Marika asked.

"Yes, I'm sure," Justine said. "Follow me."

Justine walked to the right. But the end was not there after all. So she turned onto another path. Then another. And another. Finally, she made it to the end.

"Yay! We did it!" Justine cheered. "I led us all the way here."

No one else was cheering. Justine turned around to see why everyone was so quiet.

There was nobody behind her.

"Hey, you guys!" Justine shouted. "I'm at the end. Where are you? Why aren't you following me?"

No one answered.

"Where are you?" Justine shouted even louder.

Justine looked left. She looked right. She looked back. She looked front. But the other first graders were gone!

"Oh, no!" Justine shouted. "Miss Popper! Help!"

Chapter 10
Lost and Found

Miss Popper and Mr. Barker came running over.

"What's wrong, Justine?" Miss Popper asked.

"I lost the class," Justine told her.

"Where are they?" Miss Popper asked.

"I don't know," Justine said. "That's why they're lost."

"They couldn't have gone far," Mr. Barker said.

"I looked everywhere. They just disappeared," Justine told him. "Do you think a maze monster captured them?"

"We have a lot of animals here," Mr. Barker said. "But there are no monsters."

Just then, Carlos, J.B., Albert, and Marika jumped out of the maze.

"Fooled you!" the first graders all shouted at once.

"We were hiding in the bushes," Marika said.

"We slipped away one by one," J.B. added.

"Did you like our joke?" Carlos asked her.

"It was funny, right?" Albert said.

"No!" Justine shouted. "It was *not* funny. It scared me."

"Like the snakes in the jar scared me?" Carlos asked.

"Or the worm in my apple scared *me*?" Marika added.

"It's not so funny when I'm the one being fooled," Justine admitted.

"That's what we wanted to show you," J.B. said.

"It was Albert's idea," Carlos told Justine.

Miss Popper looked sternly at Marika, Carlos, Albert, and J.B.

"That was not a nice trick," she told the class. "You didn't just scare Justine. Mr. Barker and I were worried, too. You were supposed to all stay together."

"We're sorry," Albert said.

"I'm sorry, too," Justine told Miss

Popper and her friends. "I wasn't being very nice."

"None of us were," Marika admitted.

"Are we friends again?" Justine asked her classmates.

"Yes, we are!" J.B., Albert, Carlos, and Marika cheered.

Miss Popper smiled. "Now that everyone is here, we can set our butterflies free," she said.

Mr. Barker handed her the butterfly cage. "Here you go," he said.

"Are you ready?" Miss Popper asked her class.

"If the butterflies are ready, we're ready!" Albert answered.

Miss Popper opened the top of the cage. The butterflies flew free.

"Good-bye!" Marika shouted to the butterflies.

"I'll miss them," Carlos said.

"Me, too," Albert agreed.

"Those are lucky butterflies," J.B. said. "This is a beautiful place to live."

"It sure is," Justine agreed. "And I'm not joking!"

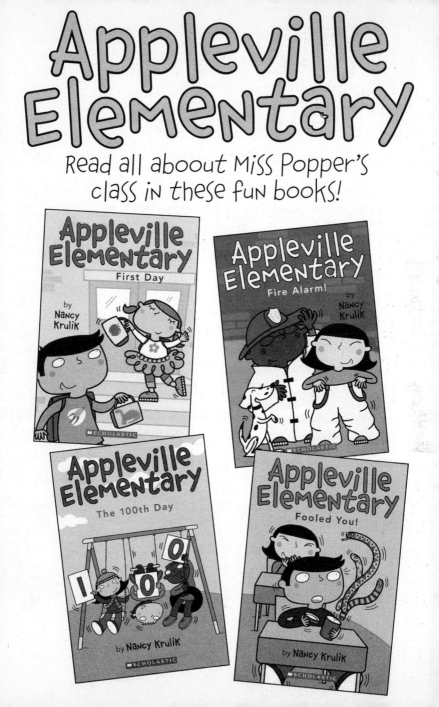